Elf Night

Jan Wahl

illustrated by Peter Weevers

Carolrhoda Books, Inc./Minneapolis

Sudden yellow moon

Splashing on the floor.

Rub your eyes.

Whispers from the door!

Kick off the covers

And wiggle your toes.

Whippoorwill calls.

Crisp breeze blows.

You forgot your slippers.

Never never mind.

Magic is calling.

Look ahead, look behind.

Be quiet. Listen!

Don't make a sound.

Put your ear

Against the ground.

The night is waking—

Bright and still.

Misty movement

Over a far hill . . .

Through wet grass

Cool and long,

You might hear

Silver tiny song.

Be quick! Hide

By the dark oak tree.

For soon they'll come,

And you will see.

Swiftly chirping,
Crickets glide.
On shiny backs,
Elf folk ride.

And prance and jump—

Dash out and in.

Toadstools turn,

While milkweeds spin.

Fireflies follow

With dancing light.

Whirling stars

Glow burning bright.

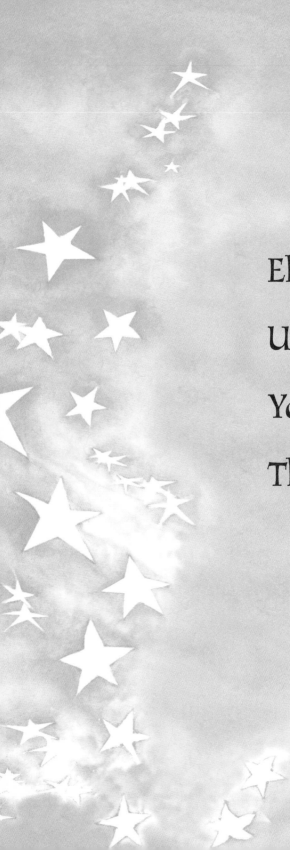

Elves are laughing.

Up and up they slide.

You can't catch them,

They will hide.

Moontime is their

Time to play—

Elves can never

Live by day.

Scary owl hoots.

He whistles to shout:

"Away. Hurry! Run!

Out, out, out!"

Through damp dew hollow

By tall oak tree,

Elves slip into

Shadows soundlessly.

Now dry your feet.

Climb back in bed.

You know they were there,

Sleepyhead.

To ROB and CAROL with love
—jw

To dreams and lost Paradises
—pw

Carolrhoda Books, Inc.
A division of Lerner Publishing Group
241 First Avenue North
Minneapolis, MN 55401 U.S.A.

Website address: www.lernerbooks.com

Library of Congress Cataloging-in-Publication Data

Wahl, Jan.
    Elf night / by Jan Wahl ; illustrated by Peter Weevers.
      p.   cm.
    Summary: At bedtime, a child enters the magical, miniature world of the elves.
    ISBN: 1-57505-512-0 (lib. bdg. : alk. paper)
    [1. Bedtime—Fiction. 2. Dreams—Fiction. 3. Elves—Fiction. 4. Lullabies.
    5. Stories in rhyme.] I. Weevers, Peter, ill. II. Title.
    PZ8.3.W133 El 2002
    [E]—dc21   2001001215

Manufactured in the United States of America
1 2 3 4 5 6 —JR—07 06 05 04 03 02